ASSISTED LIVING

by

Jim Freund

Copyright © 2024 Jim Freund

All Rights Reserved

ISBN: 9798345647738

Preface, Acknowledgements and Dedication

This is the third novella I've written in the past three years, following *The Gold-Plated Years* in 2022 and *Oh What a Tangled Web We Weave* in 2023.

The two earlier novellas were extensions of two short stories of mine that ended with things up in the air, so the task was to deal with how the major characters handled problems in the subsequent period. In *Assisted Living*, however, I liked the way the short story (of the same name) ended; so my focus was on a prequel and enriching the tale.

This novella addresses whether romance can overcome obstacles and flourish in a senior setting, with a subplot featuring the unexpected inversion of a mentor-mentee relationship.

I want to acknowledge the skillful cover illustration of my long-time collaborator, Joe Azar; the superb textual editing by my good friend, John Doyle; and the multiple tireless contributions to the finished product of my colleague Raymond.

As for a dedication, I once more turn to my wonderful wife Barbara – the principal support of this newly anointed nonagenarian, and the love of my life.

I hope you enjoy *Assisted Living*.

November 2024   Jim Freund

ASSISTED LIVING

A LOOK BACK

"Let me know if you need any help, Mr. Randolph," said the young aide on the staff of Elmwood Assisted Living as she exited his room Friday morning.

"Thank you," said Roy Randolph, sinking down into the one comfortable chair in his new residence. Roy was of medium height, trim around the waist, with a full head of gray hair and looking younger than his 82 years. He enjoyed good health, except for a case of what's called AMD – age-related macular degeneration, an eye ailment that blurs central vision.

Roy's gaze swept the contours of the small room, which contained a single bed, a closet, a clothes cabinet, some bookshelves, a desk and chair, and the armchair he now occupied. A door led to an undersized bathroom. Alongside the bed were a few unpacked suitcases and other containers holding his complete worldly possessions.

"What am I doing here?" Roy wailed to himself. But he knew damn well the answer to his mute query. He was there because he had no place else to go. In fact, he was lucky even to be here at Elmwood Assisted Living.

He slapped his cheeks to counter the self-pity, and leaned back in his chair to review the major elements that had combined to land him here: the lack of family, a minimal level of finances, an inability to land a job, and his diminished eyesight.

First was family – notable by its absence. He had no wife, no children, no living parents or siblings. His mother passed away when he was still a boy. His younger sister died at an early age. He had stayed close to his father for many years, which included a lengthy illness that required plenty of personal care from Roy, until his dad's death 20 years ago.

Roy then focused on a subject he usually avoided – the big gap in his family life that resulted from his never having married or had children. He liked women, dated many over the years, and even had some extended relationships, but ultimately none had worked out. He pondered what it was that kept him single . . .

Roy remembered an evening years back when he was dining with his cousin Alice – a woman he liked a lot and whose company he missed since her passing a decade ago. After they had shared a bottle of Sancerre, Alice began to press him as to why he never wed.

Roy had always shrugged off such inquiries with silence or wry quips. But this night the wine took over, and he recounted to Alice the reason that came back to him so vividly. Roy now decided to revisit the tale he told Alice that evening.

"Well, Alice, as you know, after college I served as an officer in the Navy on a ship stationed in Newport. During those years I entered into a very warm relationship with a lovely young woman named Paula. We spent a lot of time together when the ship was in port, which was much of the time. I was really in love and prepared to go all the way to the altar with her when my Navy stint was completed.

"At one point, a new Captain took command of the ship. His wife had remained at their home, which was

located in a different city. I was anxious to work out good relations with him, so when my friends and I decided to throw a big party at Paula's house, I invited him to join us. By coincidence, a college classmate of mine, Dick Jones, happened to be passing through the area, and I also invited him to join us.

"The party was terrific. I took on the task of introducing the Captain to everyone he didn't know – including Dick, whom I identified as "my good friend from college". The introductions included an attractive flight attendant buddy of Paula (I think her name was "Nancy"), who was there without a date.

"A half hour later, I saw the Captain canoodling with Nancy in a corner of the room, looking very happy. I was pleased. Obviously I'd already gone a long way toward getting him to appreciate me – if not for my nautical skills, then at least for my matchmaking ability.

"After that, I lost track of things while joining in a ceremony to introduce the home brew we had made in Paula's cellar. When this ended, I looked around for Dick, who seemed to have disappeared. I asked if anyone had seen him and was told by a fellow officer, "Oh, Dick left ten minutes ago with Nancy." Just then, I caught sight of the Captain, visibly angry, putting on his jacket and stalking out of the house.

"In the days following back on board ship, I detected a certain coolness in the Captain's attitude towards me. But I didn't realize how angry he was. He must have considered it an unforgivable embarrassment, to lose Nancy to a friend of mine.

> Roy recalled Alice breaking into his narrative there: "That's a helluva story Roy, but what does it have to do with your remaining single for life?" "Hang on, Alice," he had replied, "Here it comes."

> "Later that same year I took a two-week leave to visit my parents back home in Connecticut. While I was away, the Captain contacted my girl Paula, asked her out for dinner, and immediately embarked on an accelerated courtship – which included him leaving his wife for Paula and causing her to break off relations with me.

> "When that happened, I was devastated. I had every reason to believe that Paula was destined to become my lifetime partner – and then, just like that, she was gone. I considered it such a betrayal on her part, I never got over it. Although I dated other women in succeeding years, I was never able to entrust my love to anyone. And I believe that this, more than anything else, accounts for my never getting married."

The recollection of what occurred was still painful to Roy 60 years later. He shook his head vigorously, rose from his chair, and took a few laps around the room. He then busied himself with opening one of the suitcases and putting away a few of his clothes. But he soon retreated to the armchair and resumed his train of thought.

No one in his family had ever attended college; and after high school, his parents – who were anything but affluent – expected him to go to work in the small family dry goods business without attending college. But he had done well all through school and was determined to get a university degree.

He knew that paying for his college would be a real financial strain on his parents, and also mean that his younger sister would have to forego higher education. Yet he played on the pity they would feel about depriving him from the complete education needed for a successful career outside the family business. He persisted and ultimately obtained their approval. On the basis of a partial scholarship and their financial support, he ended up with a college degree.

But it was at great cost. To raise the necessary funds, his father had to redouble his workload, and the extra exertion probably created health issues that he never really overcame. And his sister, resentful of the fact that she was never able to attend college, turned bitter toward Roy, leading to a very troubled relationship between them.

Only years later did he realize how insensitive it had been for him to behave like that. He then made a silent vow that he would never again use self-pity with others to serve a goal of his own.

After leaving the Navy, Roy chose to pursue a career in teaching. His specialty was English and American literature, which he taught to high school students at a small private school in the mid-sized Connecticut town where he lived. The job didn't pay much, but his love of teaching grew, and his students held him in high regard.

At one point several decades ago, a friend had tried to induce Roy into leaving the school to join a for-profit educational company start-up – a venture that held a prospect of substantial financial rewards. Although the opportunity was attractive, Roy was unwilling to give up teaching and he turned it down. The venture proved to be successful; and he later recognized that if he had he taken the job, he might have ended up a millionaire.

Roy always claimed that this didn't bother him. Still, when a similar business opportunity arose years later, he decided to take the offer and end the long-term association with his school. But the venture didn't work out, and in fact dissipated most of Roy's meager savings.

What followed was even more dispiriting. He applied for reinstatement at the school where he'd taught successfully for so many years. The school's headmaster, never a friend, declined to take him back, citing Roy's "advanced age" and diminished eyesight. Roy was certain that the headmaster had been angry about Roy leaving the school for the second opportunity, and that this was his payback time.

With no income, Roy's immediate need then was to find an inexpensive place to live. Someone suggested that he contact Elmwood Assisted Living. Roy reacted favorably to the idea, but soon discovered that Elmwood's cost for accommodations was beyond his means.

Then he got a break. When the Elmwood staffers who interviewed Roy learned he had been an English teacher, they came up with a helpful idea. Roy could conduct regular English Lit classes for those living at Elmwood, in return for which the monthly charges would be reduced to a level he could handle. The deal was struck and his immediate problem resolved.

At this point, Roy broke off his trip down memory lane and decided to take a walk through the halls of Elmwood. The facilities were adequate, but not splashy. There was a dining room, a small library, a room to watch TV, and a place to conduct activities, such as the English class he would be teaching.

Along the way he encountered other people who were also out for a stroll, although he had yet to meet any of them. The other residents appeared to be generally in his age group, give or take a few years. They looked pleasant enough; and there was even one woman, a bit younger and rather attractive – but she was pushing a wheelchair in which was seated a man, probably her husband; and her attention seemed totally directed to making him comfortable. It reminded Roy of the care he had provided for his father in the latter's declining years.

Roy had no trouble walking the halls, but had a hard time focusing on people and places, due to the condition affecting his eyesight. It had come on gradually over the past two decades. Although he could still get around, he was no longer able to read well or manage close-up tasks. He knew this would present problems in conducting his English class, but he had developed a plan and was confident he'd be able to overcome this obstacle.

Bottom line, though, the frequent frustration caused by this condition annoyed him greatly. The worst aspect of his condition was the loss of independence. He had to be driven places; in stores where he needed to purchase items, they had to be pointed out to him; he couldn't read a restaurant menu or the credit card slip; and in many other ways, he wasn't his old self-reliant person. Still, he struggled to keep a positive attitude.

Roy checked his watch. He was expecting a visitor in a few minutes.

During his discussions with the Elmwood staff about the prospect of teaching English Lit to the residents, and aware of the problem his reduced eyesight might create. Roy had asked if they knew of anyone who could read good literature to him and otherwise help him prepare for his teaching responsibilities.

The Elmwood management found a young man whom they thought filled the bill. Eddie Andrews, 20, was a night student at the local community college, majoring in English. This sounded good to Roy, and he arranged in advance to interview Eddie on the day he moved in to Elmwood.

Sure enough, within minutes there was a knock at his door. It was Eddie. He was tall and clean-cut, seemingly intelligent, appropriately deferential to Roy, and candid in his replies to questions. Roy liked him from the outset.

Eddie's early answers indicated that he came from a family of limited means. For financial reasons, he still lived at home. He worked at a book store during the day and attended classes in the evening.

Roy cleared his throat, a gesture that often preceded him asking important questions: "Do you like good literature? – and I'm not just talking about the junk you can access on the internet?"

Eddie's reply was immediate. "I sure do. Hemingway, Fitzgerald, Faulkner – the works."

"Have you thought about your career?"

"I want to be a teacher," Eddie said – "English and American literature."

Roy smiled broadly and hired Eddie on the spot.

THE CHALLENGE

"There was music from my neighbor's house through the summer nights. . . ." Eddie, reading aloud from Roy's well-thumbed copy of *The Great Gatsby*, slowed down as he mouthed the sensuous words of the next line: "In his blue gardens men and girls came and went like moths among the whisperings and the champagne and the stars. . . ."

"Oh, yes, indeed" said Roy, his eyes closed, a warm smile wreathing his deeply-lined face. "Just listen, Eddie, to how Fitzgerald draws the reader into Gatsby's world." Then, easing back in the armchair, Roy recited the phrases from memory: 'came and went like moths' – just picture that, Eddie – and then, 'among the whisperings and the champagne and the stars' – isn't that marvelous?"

Seated in the desk chair facing Roy, two months after he had been hired, Eddie looked up from the page. "Sure is – and even better when spoken from memory."

"Well, that's just what I did for a living all those years – teaching English literature to high school students who'd been raised on comic books, and introducing them to the sound of really great prose. Most of them didn't even read the books I assigned, but simply scanned the Cliff Notes before class. So I'd recite certain passages from memory – to give them a sense of what they were missing."

He cleared his throat – a signal, Eddie recognized, that Roy was about to impart some words of wisdom. "That's an important point for you to keep in mind, Eddie, if you're going into teaching one day. An English teacher has to demonstrate how words make a difference."

Eddie nodded. "I can see that. Did you always get through to your students?"

"No, only some of them. It also depended on picking the right passages to highlight. For instance, I happen to love the epigraph to *The Great Gatsby*, written by Thomas Parke D'Invilliers, which goes like this:

> *Then wear the gold hat, if that will move her;*
> *If you can bounce high, bounce for her too,*
> *Till she cry "Lover, gold-hatted,*
> *high-bouncing lover,*
> *I must have you.'*

But I never recited that to them, because they wouldn't have known what the hell D'Invilliers was talking about. . . ."

Eddie looked bemused. "What was he talking about?"

"Aha – I've peaked your interest. We'll talk about that when you finish reading *Gatsby* to me. Now let's get back to that third chapter, with the 'five crates of oranges and lemons,' the 'salads of harlequin designs' – and then, the line I remember so well, 'The lights grow brighter as the earth lurches away from the sun' . . ."

Eddie resumed reading to Roy, who would stop him often to comment on some aspect of the novel, or to quote a line from it or from some other source he liked, or to offer a tidbit of advice. And several times a day, Roy would pass along to Eddie one of his favorite aphorisms that he'd picked up along the way, such as the most recent one – aimed at someone who wasn't carrying his weight: "When there's a piano to be moved, don't reach for the stool."

They had developed a warm relationship over several months. Although in better physical shape than many other Elmwood inhabitants, Roy needed the facility's medical support to cope with his AMD. He was still able to see well enough to get around, but he no longer could read the quality literature that filled the shelves of his small quarters, and he needed assistance in preparing to teach the English Lit course to Elmwood's inhabitants.

Each weekday in the spare hour Eddie had between the close of his day job in the bookstore and the start of his evening classes at the local community college, he would come to Elmwood to read to Roy and help him prepare for his next class. Eddie photocopied pages of the material Roy would be discussing, to be handed out to his students. Eddie could tell from Roy's enthusiastic response that these sessions with him were one of the highlights of Roy's drab life.

Roy had considered whether audio books could substitute for Eddie's "live" performance. But the prospect didn't appeal to him – he valued a live reader. You can't have a conversation with a machine, he told himself, and you can't teach someone the worthiness of the prose, like I'm doing with Eddie now. Still, his prime reason, which he didn't express, was that the interaction eased his loneliness.

Later that afternoon, when Eddie finished a description of one of Jay Gatsby's parties – "A sudden emptiness seemed to flow now from the windows and the great doors, endowing with complete isolation the figure of the host, who stood on the porch, his hand up in a formal gesture of farewell" – Roy said, "Stop there."

"But that's not the end of Chapter 3."

"I know, but there's something else I want to talk to you about."

Eddie put *Gatsby* down – a little surprised frankly, because Roy seldom conversed with him on subjects not involving literature and teaching.

Roy sat up straight and looked directly at the young man. When Roy started to speak, Eddie noticed that he didn't pause for the usual throat-clearing.

"Eddie, you know how I'm always giving you advice in our sessions – well, now I want to solicit *your* advice on a matter that's important to me. I hope you won't mind, but there's no one else to whom I might turn. The friends I used to have are either deceased or non-communicative or nowhere around; and I haven't found anyone who qualifies as a confidant among the few older men here. But I've developed a great deal of respect for your good judgment, Eddie, and I think you can help me out on this."

Eddie, caught unaware by this unexpected development, replied, "Well, I'm flattered that you're turning to me. I don't know if I can be of much help, but I'll sure give it a try."

Turning to another for advice was something Roy had seldom done in past years. He had given a lot of advice to others as a teacher, but he hadn't sought much. He hadn't even consulted any knowledgeable observer on either of the missteps he made in first spurning and later succumbing to proposals to leave teaching for business. He mused, *Maybe I would have fared better if I'd reached out for help there. And this subject today is one I haven't been too insightful on in prior years. Anyhow, here goes.*

"Okay," said Roy, "now here's the situation." This time Roy did clear his throat before proceeding. "There are many more women at Elmwood than men – we males just don't live as long as they do – and I don't mind saying, at the risk of seeming immodest, that a number of them have already shown an interest in me. For instance, there's one lady in my English class . . ." and he made a gesture signifying how uncomfortable she made him feel.

"The interest might be characterized as pre-romantic – 'pre' because I've never permitted any of their interests to endure long enough to blossom. What can I tell you? – most of these ladies are nice enough individuals, but they're either too old or infirm or lacking in intelligence or uninterested in literature to arouse my interest."

Roy paused to take a sip of coffee from a cup on the small end table. To Eddie, it seemed like Roy was revving himself up for whatever he was about to say.

"But there is one woman here –" at which point Eddie noticed Roy's face lighting up and a smile playing about his lips – "a woman named Brenda who – well, to use the vernacular – really turns me on. I spotted her in the hallway the first day I was here, but I still barely know her. I've now seen her in action in the halls and dining room, as much as I can see with these infirm eyes, and I've heard her speak – my ears still work. She's younger than most of the residents here – I'd say in her mid-70's – and she's attractive, vivacious, intelligent, humorous – the whole nine yards. And I've found out that for most of her adult life, she was a librarian – so I have no doubt we share a love of literature."

Roy paused, as if savoring his vision of Brenda. Eddie chose the moment to speak up. "Pardon me, Roy, but

Brenda sounds great. No offense, but what's she doing in this place?"

Roy nodded appreciatively. "Good question. I was just coming to that, because this is precisely where my problem lies. She's here because of her husband, Bob – that's right, she's married. He has Alzheimer's, can't take care of himself, and needs a wheelchair or moves at a painfully slow pace with a walker. From everything I observe, she's dedicated herself to Bob's care in a very loving and patient fashion, but they still need the support of the Elmwood staff to get her husband through his daily routine."

Eddie could visualize Brenda's typical day spent caring for her afflicted husband; but he said nothing, waiting for Roy to finish.

"And so, Eddie, this is my dilemma. To be crude about it, I don't think her husband is going to last very long; and I'd like to be there, close to Brenda, when poor Bob breathes his last. I'm sure there are other men around with similar ideas – there's one new guy here in particular, Larry Owen, who seems very interested in Brenda. It may sound crude, but I want to get there first."

Roy shook his head slightly, as if in wordless self-reproach for his blunt intentions, and then went on. "What I want to know, Eddie, is how I should handle this situation. I think Brenda and I could become close, but she's not reacting to me in any attentive way – not showing anything but devotion to her husband. If something is going to happen now, I have to initiate it."

Roy stopped talking, and Eddie could tell he was awaiting a response. Eddie was touched by what had just transpired – the elder Roy sharing with young Eddie what must have been an embarrassing disclosure of his intent, and then seeking Eddie's advice.

Eddie had been struck by Roy's avowal of having "a great deal of respect" for Eddie's "good judgment." It might have just been flattery, Eddie realized, but he decided to take it as a genuine compliment – mainly because he *did* think of himself that way. Since his early teens, he had worked in a series of jobs where decisions had to be made, and he'd never been found wanting. Many of these had involved dealing with, or even negotiating against, other people, so he felt right at home analyzing inter-personal matters. And he knew something about women from close proximity to his mother, his younger sisters, and his long-time girlfriend, Carla.

Eddie instinctively sensed what Roy's course of action should be, and he decided to wade in. "Well, this isn't exactly my specialty, so you can discount whatever suggestions I make, but I do have a thought that might be helpful."

"Good," said Roy, "Let me have it – that's what I'm asking for."

Eddie found himself clearing his throat – an unconscious mimicry of Roy's usual prelude to giving advice.

"I agree that you need to get closer to Brenda now – don't wait and then be edged out by one of those other fired-up guys. But you can't do it as a – what's that out-of-date word you used a few weeks back? – oh yeah, as a *lothario*. She'd be sure to resist if you were to make a pass at her."

"I'm with you on that."

"What you need to do is to become her *friend*. And what's the best way to do that? It's by offering to help out with her husband. Take Bob for walks, or recite poetry to him, or assist her at his mealtimes – I'm sure you can come up with ways to be helpful. Brenda will appreciate that – and then, when Bob exits, you'll be well-positioned as a good and supportive friend."

Roy's face broke out in a big smile. "Oh, I like that advice. It's so obvious, but I never thought of it in quite that way. And plus, it's offering to provide a useful service, which I know just how to handle, as I did with my father . . . .

"All right, Eddie, thanks a lot – I can take it from here." Roy's tone then reverted abruptly to his avuncular teacher mode. "We still have 20 minutes – let's get back to Fitzgerald, and hear the next stuff about Nick Carraway and Jordan Baker . . . ."

* * *

Shortly after arriving at Elmwood, Roy began teaching his English Lit class to the residents for an hour each on Tuesday and Thursday afternoons. The course concentrated on American novelists and poets, which had been Roy's classroom specialty in his former profession.

The first few sessions were sparsely attended, but as word spread about how entertaining Roy was, attendance picked up a lot. The bulk of the audience consisted of women – but then, after all, a solid majority of the Elmwood residents were widows.

Roy had no extra books to distribute, but when there

was a particular bit of prose that he wanted them to read, Eddie would photocopy the relevant pages from Roy's little library. As for poetry, Roy had previously memorized many of the pertinent excerpts and could deliver them by heart with appropriate feeling.

Here, for example, are a few excerpts from an early poetry session, which featured the 19th century New England poet Emily Dickinson, one of Roy's favorites. He spoke without notes.

"Her best-known poems dealt with death and the afterlife. Here's a prime example.

*"Because I could not stop for Death –
He kindly stopped for me –
The carriage held but just ourselves –
And immortality.*

Then Roy switched from meditative to hopeful. "Dickinson could also be life-affirming, as in *'Hope is the thing with feathers / that perches in the soul / and sings the tune without the words – and never stops at all.'* But she doesn't stop there – and she concludes with her highest praise for hope (which Roy delivered slowly and with appropriate feeling): *'It never asked a crumb of me.'* "

From there, he changed the emphasis to display her flexibility. "Many of Dickinson's poems were on the subject of fame. Perhaps the most notable she titled "*Success is Counted Sweetest,*" and the first line tells it all: *Success is counted sweetest / by those who ne'er succeed.*' "As for those who have some success but aren't satisfied with it, just listen to the poem's last line: *'As he defeated-dying / on whose forbidden ear / the distant strains of triumph / burst agonized and clear.'* "

* * *

"That would be good both going and coming back / One could do worse than be a swinger of birches."

It was a month later. Roy opened his eyes as he finished reciting the poem he'd committed to memory so many years ago. "Don't you enjoy *Birches*, Bob? It's one of Frost's finest."

Brenda's husband, Bob, sat in a reclining chair in the living room of their quarters at Elmwood. He was staring out into space, a blank expression on his face, and made no attempt to reply. Roy, seated on a pull-up chair near Bob, waited a moment – although not expecting a response – and then continued.

"Here's another of Frost's poems that I fancy. It has two famous lines that oppose each other – the first line, 'Something there is that doesn't love a wall,' and the last line, 'Good fences make good neighbors.' "

At that moment, the outer door of the apartment opened and Brenda came in, carrying a small plastic bag that displayed the logo of the neighborhood drugstore.

"Well, hello, you two," she said – "and since I could hear your voice through the door, Roy, I realize I've just interrupted your recital of Frost's *Mending Wall*. It was my favorite poem freshman year in college. . . . You guys seem to be getting along splendidly – am I right, Bob?"

Bob's expression had changed to a faint smile upon sensing Brenda's presence, but he showed no sign of responding to her inquiry, nor had she expected any. While removing her coat and emptying the contents of the bag, she spoke to Roy as if Bob weren't in the room.

"I can't tell you how pleased I am, Roy, that you volunteered to spend some time with Bob – to recite those wonderful poems, to take him for walks, and so many other kindnesses. He may not show you his appreciation, but I'm sure that deep down he's as grateful as I am – and I certainly am, because it frees me up to run some necessary errands and get off by myself for a bit."

"Thanks, Brenda, but you left out the fact that it's also beneficial for *me* – testing my memory on the old verses, getting some exercise myself. Most of all, I'm experiencing the good feeling that comes with being of help to someone who needs assistance."

"You're a lovely man, Roy. I'm awed at how well you deal with your own eyesight problem and manage to enjoy a normal, even youthful, existence. . . . ."

* * *

A week later, Roy and Bob came to a stop outside Bob's apartment. Brenda opened the door in response to their knock. Roy steered Bob and his walker at a slow pace over to the reclining chair. Roy then joined Brenda, who was preparing a meal in the small kitchen.

Brenda looked up and said, "Thanks, Roy, for getting Bob up on his feet – he needed that."

"Happy to do it. By the way, did you see the announcement that they're going to have a string quartet on Saturday in the auditorium – playing some Schubert, I believe."

"Oh, a favorite of mine."

"Me, too. Well, if you'd like to go, I'll come over here an hour earlier, so we can prepare Bob and help him get over there and into our seats before the crowd comes in."

"That would be terrific. Roy, I don't know what I'd do without you."

* * *

But several weeks later, when Brenda answered the phone, Roy could tell something was wrong.

"Hi, Brenda – I was just thinking I hadn't seen you and Bob for a few days –"

Brenda interrupted. "Bob has taken a turn for the worse. The doctor was here earlier today." Her voice was clearly troubled.

"Oh, I'm so sorry – is there anything I can do?"

"Not at the moment, but thanks for asking."

* * *

The next time Roy saw Brenda was a few days later, on a Saturday, at a funeral service for Bob being held in Elmwood's small chapel. He offered her his condolences, and they shared a hug of friendship; but with a number of other people around, the two of them had no time alone to talk.

* * *

"So," said Eddie to Roy at the beginning of their

session the following Monday, "we've finished *The Sun Also Rises*. We can talk a little about Jake's malady or Brett's lust, or we can just move on to Faulkner."

Roy, who was sitting in his desk chair, smiled. "We'll get to Jake and Brett in a few minutes. But first I want to ask your advice again."

"Okay, shoot" – and here Eddie smiled impishly – "but I warn you, I may have to raise my hourly fee for this unexpected use of my brain."

"Consider it done." Roy cleared his throat. "So Eddie, as you may have heard, Brenda's husband passed away last week. I paid my respects as a friend should, but now I want to move on with my pursuit of Brenda. And the question is how I should go about it. Do I now play the paramour?"

Over the weekend, Eddie had learned of Bob's passing, so he wasn't surprised by Roy's line of inquiry. Eddie had been pleased that his first venture into advising Roy on matters of the heart went so well, which bolstered his self-confidence – not only in dealing with Roy, but in other areas of his life as well.

By way of example, Eddie had begun exploring the possibility of transferring from the small community college he attended to the large state university fifty miles away. The prospect was exciting to him, and any doubts he formerly had regarding his ability to make the transition were rapidly eroding. He knew his parents wouldn't be able to help him financially, but he had some savings from his current job and assumed he could find part-time work in the new location. The main obstacle was leaving Roy. Eddie was not only stimulated by what Roy was able to offer him in terms of a special education, but he had developed a genuine affection for him.

Eddie had no hesitation about responding to Roy's question, since he instantly sensed that Roy's playing "paramour" would be the wrong course to take.

"No, no," said Eddie, "don't come on too strong. You have to build on what you've created these past months. You're a close friend of the family – you can't suddenly become a lover. Just be a fellow mourner."

Noting Roy's rapt attention, Eddie paused to let the concept sink in before proceeding in a confident tone. "This is a big change in Brenda's life, and she needs time to adjust to it. You've got to help her through this period without seeming to have any impure intentions. Play your cards right, and then, when the right time comes – which, don't worry, you'll know – make your move...."

* * *

"These cashmere sweaters," said Roy a week later, pointing to a drawer in Bob's bedroom dresser, "are too good to discard. They should go to the Salvation Army, or perhaps to some of the men living at Elmwood."

"You're right," said Brenda from her desk on the other side of the room. "Oh, it's so helpful to have you go through Bob's clothes and belongings with me – bringing a man's eye to these decisions...."

* * *

One Sunday morning not long after that, Roy and Brenda were standing in the alcove at the rear of the local church as the parishioners filed out following the service.

"Roy, that was such a good idea for us to attend church this morning."

"I thought it might be, when I heard what the subject of the sermon was going to be."

"Yes, and the pastor had such a helpful approach on how to deal with grief. . . ."

* * *

A month after Bob's passing, Brenda and Roy were standing outside the door to Brenda's apartment. She put her key in the lock and opened the door part way, then turned to Roy and clasped one of his hands with both of hers.

"Thanks so much for taking me to the concert tonight. The music was excellent, and it did me a world of good to get out of this apartment for a change."

Roy placed his other hand over Brenda's and said, "I too enjoyed it thoroughly."

"Well," she said after a few moments, extricating her hands from his and turning to enter the apartment, "good night Roy."

"Good night, Brenda," he said and turned to go back to his quarters – a little disappointed that the hand-clasp hadn't accelerated some mutual passion, but satisfied that he'd avoided any premature rush to intimacy.

* * *

The next day, Roy was walking in the Elmwood hallway for exercise. He was about to turn a corner when he heard Brenda's voice coming from the other side of the wall.

"Oh, yes, Larry, that would be fun. And I do so enjoy Woody Allen movies."

Roy stopped in his tracks. Then he heard a man's voice, saying, "Fine. I'll pick you up at your place at six, so we can grab a bite before the picture starts. See you tonight."

A moment later, the man behind the voice turned the corner, walking toward Roy and nodding a brief impersonal hello as he passed. Roy nodded back but stayed where he was, not wanting to encounter Brenda just then.

The man, Roy knew, was Larry Owen, who had arrived at Elmwood earlier that year. He appeared to be in his 70's, good-looking, in possession of all his faculties, and walking with a brisk stride. Roy had noticed Larry and Brenda being together on several occasions, including a session at the bridge table in Elmwood's lounge. . . .

* * *

"I don't know, Eddie," said Roy that afternoon, "whether our strategy is working."

"Just be patient," replied Eddie – "remember the words of Edmund Burke that you taught me, 'Never despair, but if you do, work on in despair'."

Roy smiled, pleased that Eddie recalled one of his favorite lines. "Touché – I will do just that. But I'm worried about this fellow Larry Owen, who's been paying a lot of attention to Brenda since Bob's death. He seems to have some positive assets, including flawless eyesight. . . . And they play bridge together, a game I never liked – give me Scrabble any time. I've also heard he's a fine dancer, while I'm something of a klutz in that department."

He paused for a moment, realizing the situation reminded him of how he had lost his girl Paula to that damn Captain so many years ago. He wasn't about to let that happen this time. " Eddie, I don't want to miss out on Brenda by holding off too long."

"Don't worry about the competition. Just recall one of your favorite sayings – that a kite rises against, not with the wind. As for timing, I've always said that you'll know when the right moment comes. . . ."

Notwithstanding Eddie's seeming nonchalance about Roy's "rival", Roy decided he needed to find out more about Larry Owen. So the next time he saw Larry in the hall, Roy introduced himself and suggested they ought to get to know each other. They made a lunch date, which went well and led to several other get-togethers. As time passed, Larry opened up to him about his life.

At one of their lunches, Roy said to Larry, "I'm interested in what you – a relatively young guy in seemingly good shape – is doing at this place."

Larry replied, "Well, it's a long story."

"No problem," said Roy, "I've got plenty of time."

Larry told him briefly about his early life, culminating in a first marriage that didn't work out at all. "Then," said Larry, "I next married a woman who had a lot of money. I have to say it was like a godsend; and I'm forced to admit that because of her money, I never bothered to get a serious job. Then one day, she decided to sue me for divorce."

Roy sympathized. "I'm sorry to hear that."

Larry continued, "We had a teenage daughter who I loved, but my wife wouldn't let me see her – she actually got a court order of protection against me coming near the kid. Well, I busted it – which led to a big brouhaha – they were actually going to throw me in jail."

Roy said, "That's terrible".

Larry nodded, "Eventually, we reached a compromise. She would drop the charges, if I moved away and never bothered them again. I agreed to move, but had no money to live in a decent place. She said she would support my room and board – but not a dime extra – if I came to Elmwood, which she had heard was an okay place. And so I did."

* * *

Roy now knew he had a weapon to use against Larry, but the question was how to do it. He consulted his love-life advisor, Eddie.

After relating the story to Eddie, Roy said, "So I'm just going to tell Brenda that Larry is a bad guy, and here's why she should stay away from him."

Eddie cautioned him. "No, no – you have to be more subtle about this . . . ."

"How so?" asked Roy.

Eddie thought for a few moments and then said, "Don't mention Larry's name to Brenda. Just tell her you were lunching with a guy who looked a little young for this place and asked him how come he was here." Eddie then imitated what Roy should say next to Brenda: "And Brenda, you should have heard the story he told me, involving possible jail time, his treatment of women, and his adverse financial condition."

Roy interrupted: "But how does she know it's Larry Allen I'm talking about?"

Eddie replied, "Along the way, you drop in some facts you've learned about Larry – where he went to school, what sports he likes, what countries he's visited, that he plays bridge, etc. Presumably he's told her about such things, so she can figure out herself who it was without you even mentioning his name. She'll get it – and she doesn't even have to suffer the embarrassment of needing to mention that she knows him. Believe me, Roy, Larry is dead meat after that."

Roy said, "I love it".

And the next day he used the tactic with Brenda. It definitely worked – he could tell by her reaction and expression that she knew he was referring to Larry. After that, Roy never saw Brenda with Larry even once again.

* * *

"Eddie" said Roy to him in their next session," there's been a development with Brenda that I want to run by you. Last night, we were seated side-by-side on her couch watching television. During a commercial, she turned to me and said, "Roy, I'm almost embarrassed to ask you this, but

I've got a terrible itch in the middle of my spine. Would you mind terribly scratching my back?" I complied, which evidently relieved the itch, and she said 'thank you,' and we resumed watching the television show."

Eddie said, "And that was it?"

"Yes," Roy replied, "that was it for last evening." He raised his voice as he continued. " But unless you advise me otherwise, I'm taking this as a sign that the time has come to make my move."

Eddie smiled and spread his hands in the gesture a baseball umpire uses at home plate to signal that a runner is safe. "Hey, if you think this is the right time, then go for it!"

Roy smiled, and gave Eddie a thumbs up on his go-ahead signal.

* * *

They proceeded with their session that day, but as time passed Roy noticed that Eddie seemed down in the dumps, not his usual cheerful self. Roy asked Eddie what, if anything, was wrong.

Eddie said, "Well it's not really a big deal, but the problem involves a teacher at the school I go to."

Roy replied, "Hey, Eddie, if there's one thing I know something about, it's teachers. You've helped me on these other matters – maybe I can return the favor on this one."

Eddie took up Roy's offer and spelled out the problem. In Eddie's view, the teacher (a Mr. Burns) had it in for him over something that happened a while ago; and he surmised that this was why Burns gave him a low mark on a paper Eddie had recently written – a paper that Eddie considered a good effort.

Roy asked, "Well, what do you intend to do about it?"

Eddie replied, "I'm going to tell him that I think the low mark he gave me was unfair based on the quality of my paper. Then I'll say that whatever it is that Burns doesn't like about me shouldn't have an adverse impact on my mark. And what the hell, I intend to get a little angry to show the depth of my feeling. . . . Do you agree with that approach?"

Roy said, "Well, that's one way to handle it, but it's not what I would recommend."

Eddie asked, "Well, what would you do?"

Roy asked Eddie to tell him a little about Burns, which Eddie did. Burns didn't seem to Roy like such an ogre, and he worried that Burns might react badly to the accusation Eddie intended to make. One pertinent fact that Roy noted in Eddie's description of Burns was that the teacher was a big basketball fan.

Roy then proceeded to advise Eddie. "Instead of confronting Burns directly, you might try this with him. Tell him that you'd like to get to know him better and to understand what he's looking for from his students. Then say, 'By the way, I know you're a basketball fan, and I happen to have two tickets to the big home game tomorrow night. My buddy, who was going to use the second ticket, just told me that he can't make it. How about we have an early meal at the diner and take in the game?' "

Eddie's face broke into a grin. "Good idea! Thanks, Roy, I'll definitely try it."

* * *

Late the next Sunday morning, Brenda and Roy were seated side-by-side on Brenda's sofa, having enjoyed a tasty brunch she had prepared for him. Brenda was flipping through the pages of a newspaper, calling his attention to certain articles of interest that he was unable to read himself.

Roy turned sideways to face her and cleared his throat. "Brenda, do you recall asking me a few weeks ago what my favorite lines were from Robert Frost?"

"I do," she replied, "and you said there were so many, you'd have to think about it."

"Right. Well, I've given it some thought, and now I have an answer. It's not so much the beauty of the words, but the fact that these lines capture just what I want to say at this moment."

She looked over at him, her expression a bit quizzical.

"It's the last five lines in the poem, *The Road Not Taken*. Maybe you recall them.

'I shall be telling this with a sigh
Somewhere ages and ages hence.
Two roads diverged in a wood, and I –
I took the one less traveled by,'

Here, Roy paused for emphasis, looked squarely at Brenda, and spoke the last line slowly.

'And that has made all the difference'."

She faced him, her face flushing slightly, and said in a mock-formal voice, "And to what road, Roy, do you now have reference?"

He moved as if in slow motion, putting his arm around her shoulder, gently drawing her towards him. In a near-whisper, he said, "Years hence, I want to look back on today as having been when I took the road that made all the difference in my life – the day I told my sweet Brenda how much I love her."

Brenda put her hand on the side of Roy's face, half-closed her eyes, and whispered to him, "Darling, you have just given me what Frost himself, at JFK's inauguration, called *The Gift Outright*...."

* * *

When Eddie came to his room the next evening, he reported how well Roy's advice worked out with Mr. Burns. They had enjoyed dinner and the game, and Burns voiced encouraging words to Eddie regarding his future.

Roy was exultant – but *not* about that.... "It worked! I took the risk, Eddie, and she responded beautifully. We are now, shall I say, a couple! I couldn't be happier.... Put away that book – this is no time for Faulkner. Let's switch to something humorous, to Twain, or Thurber – or better still, Bruce Jay Friedman...."

THE COUPLE

Later that night, Roy and Brenda lay quietly on his

bed together, holding hands, listening to Sinatra's voice on Roy's stereo, singing, "In the Wee Small Hours of the Morning"....

At some point, Brenda fell asleep. Roy lay there awake, his mind drifting back to that evening a decade ago when his cousin Alice pressed him as to why he'd never married. But unlike his ditching by Paula, he realized that this new and wonderful romance with Brenda had a very good chance of leading to marriage. He wondered whether he could make it all the way this time.

The answer was clear to him. That damn Paula had committed a humiliating betrayal, something that Brenda would never do. He may have been justified in letting that hold him back from considering marriage with other women he'd known, but what he was feeling for Brenda represented a completely different emotion.

He also was certain that Brenda was genuine – not phony, the real thing. He had heard many of the Elmwood residents sing her praises. No one had anything negative to say about her – all vouched for her good character.

He decided that it was time to get over being spurned years ago, and to let his relationship with Brenda blossom – hopefully to include marrying this wonderful woman.

* * *

The next evening, Brenda and Roy ate dinner in a cozy Italian restaurant. Their eyes met and their lips puckered as they toasted each other and their newly-formed bond. Roy enthused over the great stroke of luck that had brought him to Elmwood and provided the opportunity to meet her.

Roy then broadened the point. "Whenever something significant like this happens to me – and let me be clear: I can't think of anything as significant as this occurring in the last hundred years! – I'm struck by how many coincidences and other events outside my control have to occur in order for the fateful encounter or event to take place. I like to call the process *Sheer Happenstance*."

Brenda replied, "I know just what you're talking about – I feel the exact same way."

Roy continued. "And I'm *not* talking about the vagaries of fate that may affect us – hitting the big lottery number, the onset of a dreaded disease, lightning striking the tree limb we're perched under – the kind of stuff over which we have little control."

Brenda replied, "Yes – and what's fascinating is how our voluntary decisions propel us in directions which lead to relationships and outcomes that wouldn't occur without those choices we make – but then can cause all the difference in terms of our future years. Which, of course, brings us right back to Frost's fork in *The Road Not Taken*."

Roy nodded. "And that always brings to mind Yogi Berra's unassailable dictum – 'When you arrive at a fork in the road, take it.'"

Brenda chuckled and then said, "For me, the key to the poem is that, to the narrator, the two roads looked really about the same; and although he 'kept the first for another day,' he also knew full well 'how way leads on to way,' and thus doubted whether he "should ever come back.' That's just how it is in life – one thing leads to another, and then it's often difficult to retrace your steps."

Roy said, "No retracing these steps, honey" and lovingly touched her cheek.

"Some day,' Brenda said, "I'll tell you all about the many twists and turns that I went through before finally meeting and marrying Bob."

"I'll look forward to that," Roy replied. "But we've never even discussed what your marriage to Bob was like for you – both before and after he developed Alzheimers."

Brenda gave a sad shake of her head. "I've not wanted to discuss that with you – it's too close right now. And I appreciate that you've respected my privacy and didn't inquire. All I can tell you at this point – and I will go into it in more detail after a little more time has passed – is that it was a good marriage; and then, when the disease hit, it became a troubled marriage; but I'm proud of the fact that I stuck it out."

"You sure did," said Roy, placing his hand softly atop hers on the table. "I was so impressed with how you handled such a difficult situation."

"I appreciate that," she said with real warmth.

After a short pause, Roy said, "Getting back to 'sheer happenstance,' I remember well that Longfellow wrote about 'possibilities and things that do not happen;' and he summed it up by concluding – I've never forgotten his words – 'We may let slip some great occasions of good, or avoid some impending evil, by which the whole current of our lives would have been changed.' "

Brenda said, "I recall his take on this, if not the precise language – but I also remember that he never wavered in his faith."

"Right," said Roy – "and again, in his words, 'There is no possible solution to this dark enigma but one word, 'Providence'."

Brenda smiled and said, "No offense, Henry Wadsworth, but I'm more in the Frost camp, emphasizing the role of human choice."

"I'm with you," said Roy, "but I don't like to get into whether what seems like sheer happenstance is actually part of some larger plan. Still I can't resist making the observation that if some superior being is indeed pulling the strings behind all this, he (or she!) does work in some mighty mysterious and complex ways . . . ."

Now it was Brenda's turn to smile, caress Roy's face, and breathe an emotional sigh.

After a few moments, Roy returned once more to the theme of their conversation. "By the way, it's not only a voluntary decision on your part to do something, like take the fork in the road. It can also be a decision *not* to do something that comes your way. That was my decision, which I told you about, *not* to leave teaching for that first rich opportunity I was offered, thereby missing out on some profitable good fortune. I then managed to touch all the bases by my later *affirmative* decision to leave teaching for that second opportunity, which turned out so negatively."

"I agree," said Brenda. "And it can also be because someone else *didn't choose you* for what you wanted. Look at me – I became a librarian because I was turned down for a particular teaching opportunity I had yearned for."

Roy said, "I don't understand how anyone in their right mind could turn you down – but speaking of turndowns, how about the private school's refusal to rehire me when I wanted to return to teaching after my corporate opportunity didn't work out. And yet that turndown, thank the Lord, took me to Elmwood, which led me right to you."

Brenda blew him a kiss and then said, "One of my favorite Michel Legrand songs is *On my Way to You*. It's a love song for people who end up in the right romantic place, but who may rue or regret some of the choices they made along the way. The Alan and Marilyn Bergman lyric is something special."

She reached into her large pocketbook and pulled out a slip of paper. "Believe it or not, I liked it so much I made a copy of the words and carry it around with me. Here's how it goes," and she proceeded to read the lyrics aloud:

> *So often as I wait for sleep / I find myself reciting / the words I've said or would have said, / like scenes that need rewriting. / The smiles I never answered, / doors perhaps I should have opened, / songs forgotten in the morning. // I relive the roles I've played, / the tears I may have squandered; / the many pipers I have paid / along the roads I've wandered. // Yet all the time I knew it, / love was somewhere out there waiting. / Though I may regret a step or two, / if I had changed a single day, / what went amiss or went astray, / I may have never found my way to you. / I wouldn't change a thing that happened / on my way to you."*

And Roy echoed those final words, as Brenda nodded in agreement. "I wouldn't change a thing that happened on my way to *you* . . . ."

* * *

Since Roy arrived at Elmwood, Eddie had been meeting with him regularly every Monday through Friday in the late afternoon. On a recent Friday, however, Eddie failed to show up, without alerting Roy to the fact that he would be missing their session. Nor did he get in touch with Roy over the weekend to clarify his absence.

This was unlike Eddie's past performance, which had been quite reliable and the subject of Roy's periodic compliments. So when Eddie showed up the following Monday, Roy was puzzled and somewhat annoyed.

"Eddie," said Roy, "What happened to cause you to miss our Friday meeting?"

Eddie gazed down at the floor as he replied. "It was all the fault of my History professor. After our class Friday morning, he said I needed some extra work and told me to come see him late that afternoon. I just couldn't be in two places at once."

"I understand the problem," said Roy. "But why couldn't you call to alert me?"

At that point Eddie's narrative turned more and more complicated, with the blame increasingly shifted on to others. It seemed clear to Roy that whatever the real reason was, Eddie had simply made a decision Friday not to contact him; and now he was obviously reluctant to admit his oversight and apologize.

"Eddie," said Roy, "Let me offer you some advice. When you make a mistake and later realize you've done so, own up to it. Don't dream up stories and blame others. Admit what happened, apologize if someone was harmed or inconvenienced by it, and learn from what's happened so that it won't occur again."

Roy paused at that point. He could see Eddie trying to decide whether to cling to his false narrative, or whether to admit and apologize for the error.

As for Roy, he had decided that Eddie's handling of the situation was too serious to just let pass. The young man needed to receive something memorable in the nature of father-son advice, and for this Roy turned to an unforgettable incident in his own life.

So, before Eddie said anything in reply, Roy continued. "Eddie, I've been impressed by you up to now; and along the way, you've given me some very worthwhile advice. Now I'd like to return the favor by giving you some advice that will stand you in good stead for the rest of your life. I consider it so important for you to absorb this lesson that I'm going to tell you a true story about myself that makes the point visually and will be something you're unlikely to forget."

Eddie, seemingly relieved that he wouldn't have to speak up just yet, nodded to indicate he awaited the story.

Roy began with the background facts. "About ten years ago, just before my eyesight began to worsen, I was very interested in photography. I used to shoot mainly on the weekends and was always on the lookout for a good subject.

"After an overnight snowfall one Friday, I was out with my digital camera Saturday morning, looking for subjects to shoot. Suddenly something caught my eye. It was an old woman in a tattered cloth coat and galoshes, a brown shawl pulled tight over her head against the elements, trying to push a grocery cart with difficulty through the slushy remains of the snow. It was just the kind of scene I'd been hoping for all morning.

"I raised the camera to my eye, zoomed the lens in close on the woman, and snapped the first picture. Bingo! I said to myself, visualizing the poignant image that would emerge. But as I changed the angle slightly for the next shot, I noticed that the old woman had turned her head and was looking directly at me, a frown showing on her face.

"I immediately lowered the camera to my chest, trying to give the impression that I hadn't yet taken a picture but was just making the necessary preparations. Then I walked over to where the old woman was struggling with the cart and spoke to her, making my voice as respectful as possible.

"I said, 'Hello, ma'am. My name is Roy Randolph. Would you mind if I take a few pictures of you?'

"For a few moments, the old woman continued her slow progress through the slush without responding to my question. Then she stopped and straightened her body up to its full five foot-two inch height.

"She said, 'I tell you what, mister photographer. I live over there across the street, a few doors down. As you can see, I'm having trouble getting there in this rotten slush. Help me push the cart home, and then we'll talk about the pictures.'

"I realized it would be churlish to refuse her assistance. 'By all means,' I replied, letting the camera dangle around my neck and taking hold of the cart handle. As I began to push, the old woman kept one hand on the cart – more for balance, I thought, then out of fear I might run off with her groceries.

"After a few minutes, we reached the front door of an old tenement building she identified as hers. I hope you don't mind, Eddie, if I take a few minutes to describe the scene – it's as clear in my mind as if it happened yesterday."

Eddie gave a permissive nod.

Roy continued. "The tiny elevator took us to the third floor, where we exited to a narrow hall. A bright uncovered bulb exposed the peeling paint on the walls. The old woman's apartment was half-way down the hall.

"Inside, the single room was dim, and the two lamps she turned on didn't do much to brighten it. The air smelled of disinfectant. There was a threadbare couch with white crocheted doilies on its arms. A small TV sat in the corner with a rabbit-ears antenna on top. Next to the bed was a portable potty.

"I wheeled the cart to the small kitchen area. Looking up, I was surprised to see a number of professional-looking black-and-white framed photos of city scenes on the walls around the room.

"The old woman went through a slow process of removing her coat, shawl and galoshes. She motioned me to sit on the couch, while she took a nearby chair.

"When she spoke, her voice was weak but audible. 'Welcome to my little apartment, Mr. Randolph, and thank you for helping with the groceries. My name is Madge Brody. I used to be an elementary school teacher, but that was a long time ago.'

"I nodded my head and was about to tell her I was also a teacher, but realizing that she had something to say, I didn't interrupt.

"She went on. 'Here's what I think, Mr. Randolph. I know why you want to photograph me trying to push the grocery cart in the snow. I have a photographic eye, you know. Look at these fine pictures on my walls. For years they hung in my classroom. I used to say to the children that a good picture tells the truth better than a thousand words.' She closed her eyes, seemingly recalling those distant school days.

"After a few moments, she opened her eyes and went on. 'So, Mr. Randolph, down there in the snow, you wanted to show a weak, pathetic figure, overcome by the elements. You're trying to play on the sympathy of anyone viewing your photos. I'm right, aren't I?'

"She was right, of course, and I knew better than to argue the point. So I said, 'Well, I wouldn't put it in those exact words, but yes, I guess that was sort of my intention.'

"Madge Brody waggled a finger at me. 'You should be ashamed of yourself,' she said, shaking her head slowly from side to side in disapproval. Then she stopped the shaking and said with emphasis, 'But at least you're honest and admitted it.'

She then looked down at her swollen feet. 'Yes, Mr. Randolph, I'm an old woman, and I have trouble getting around.' She looked directly at me. 'But wouldn't it be nicer to take my picture doing something I can still do well, instead of struggling out there in the snow?'

"Madge treated her question as rhetorical and didn't wait for a reply before continuing. 'For instance, how about something like cooking. I happen to still be a very good cook, when I put my mind to it. And my nephew is coming over for dinner tonight, which is why I was out shopping in this terrible weather. How about it, Mr. Randolph – why don't you show me *that* way – in command in my kitchen?'

"And then she got to her feet with some difficulty, pointed to my equipment on the couch, and said, 'Get your camera and come with me.'

"Using a walker that was by the couch, she led the way to the tiny kitchen. I followed behind, not knowing how this would pan out, but I was taken with Madge and decided to go along with her proposal.

"Madge took the brown paper bags out of the grocery cart and emptied their contents onto the small counter. She put on an apron and began to engage in a painfully slow motion series of activities – chopping vegetables, scrubbing potatoes, turning on burners, poking around in the undersized oven.

"I snapped away as she worked, getting several dozen pictures. They were okay, but the real photo story here, I thought, would be to *videotape* Madge Brody's sluggish movements, so a viewer could see how long each simple chore took her to accomplish.

"At one point, Madge said, 'I don't do this so often now – only when I'm going to have company. And the arthritis in my hands slows me down. But I can still get around in the kitchen – don't you think?'

"What could I say but, 'I'm very impressed.' And indeed, I was impressed by her determination, although at the same time saddened by the seeming enormity of the task she had undertaken.

"After some time, Madge turned to me and asked, 'Is that one of those digital cameras you're using – where you can see the picture you just took?' When I nodded yes, she said, 'Well, let's see what they look like.'

"The two of us stood side-by-side against the chopping counter, our faces close to the small screen on the back of my camera, viewing the pictures in the reverse order they'd been taken. At the risk of being immodest, I'd captured the essence of the old woman in her kitchen, performing the various tasks she prided herself on. By touching a button on the back of the camera, I was able to enlarge portions of the images for closer scrutiny.

"Madge took a lively interest in the photos, peering at them closely through her thick glasses, requesting me to enlarge the picture from time to time. But she held off venturing any opinions, presumably until having seen them all.

"I didn't realize when I'd reached the last of the kitchen pictures, and I touched the photo review button one more time. The single unauthorized photo I'd snapped of the old woman in the snow now filled the small screen. I quickly tried to reverse direction to the kitchen shots, but Madge had seen the outdoor image and said with some force, 'Wait.' So I did.

"The old woman took off her glasses and reached for a magnifying glass that she kept near her recipe books. For a full minute, she closely examined the picture of herself struggling in the slush. Then, closing her eyes, she slowly nodded her head several times, as if agreeing with some inner determination she had reached.

"She put down the magnifying glass and, without saying a word, took several of the empty brown paper grocery bags and placed them back in the cart. Using the cart to steady her steps, she walked to where she'd left her outerwear. She sat down on a chair and began to pull on her galoshes. Then, turning to me, Madge Brody said in a matter-of-fact voice, 'What do you say, Mr. Randolph, we go back down to the street' – and she began to push her cart toward the door."

Roy stopped talking and nodded, to signify that this was the end of the story. He could tell from Eddie's expression that Madge's reaction had caught him by surprise – just as it had stunned Roy on that snowy day.

"Now, Eddie, before I discuss the real point of my telling you this story, I have a collateral question for you – *why* do you think Madge Brody decided to go back out in the snow?"

Eddie thought for a few moments and then said, "I remember what Madge said earlier in your story, that she had a 'photographic eye?' My hunch is that she realized the single snow picture was better than the kitchen ones, although another snow shot could be even better; and that posing for a good picture was more important to her than the nuisance of putting on her coat and galoshes again.

Roy said, "That's quite a good interpretation."

Eddie added. "Here's another thought as to what I believe the old woman might have thought when she looked at the street photo. To someone else, this photo would just have been a pathetic figure on a bad day. What she saw when she looked at it was – Madge Brody."

"Another interesting thought," said Roy. "I'm just going to add one element that I think was significant to her. Madge originally considered the snow picture of her as standing for someone who was impotent against the elements. When she actually viewed the image, she realized – with her 'photographic eye,' if you will – that there could be another way to look at it. With a few changes in her demeanor and posture, the street photos to come could depict an old woman who was struggling mightily against the elements – not giving up but bravely fighting on. And somehow she sensed that the inner determination she was exhibiting by putting back on her winter gear and going down to the cold street was precisely the kind of determination that she could exhibit in the photos – the two things matched perfectly."

Eddie nodded his head affirmatively, "I can see that."

Roy said, "The *photographic* point to the story is that by just making some subtle changes in the elements of a photo, you can create an image that projects a different and better message to the viewer. The *analytical* point to the story is that there can often be several different interpretations of a person's conduct. It's what I used to tell my younger sister, when she would analyze a complex situation with absolute assurance, and I'd say: 'That's okay, but there's another way to look at it.' Roy then paused before he added, "But neither of those points is why I told you the story, nor what I want you to take away from it."

Eddie perked up as Roy continued, "The key here occurs twice. Once when Madge tells me she knew what I had been up to. I could have lied and denied any such intention, but I didn't. I confessed that she was right, and she acknowledged that when she said, 'It was terrible but at least you were honest and admitted it.' That was crucial to our relationship continuing and led to the unexpected ending. And that's the obvious point I want to make here to you about not showing up Friday, not contacting me, and then giving me a phony story. Always tell the truth, as much as it hurts."

Eddie started to reply, but before he could, Roy went on with his analysis.

"But that was actually the lesser admission of the story. The key here was Madge Brody. When she saw the picture of herself in the snow, she realized it was better than the shots of her cooking. And Madge wasn't afraid to admit that she had been wrong about asking me to switch to photographing the cooking. Her admission wasn't conveyed by words of apology, and it didn't have to be. It was her *tacit* acknowledgement of it – re-loading the cart and putting her galoshes back on – that impressed me so much, and I hope it does you too."

"It does." Eddie said. "I'm glad you told me that story, and I definitely get your point. It was true that the reason for my not showing up Friday was the History professor's insistence on seeing me at our usual time. But even though I knew I should have called you to explain why

I was unable to come, I just couldn't get myself to do it – I knew you would be disappointed – you had told me the day before that we would be reading one of your favorite stories at the Friday session . . . ."

And the words then tumbled out of Eddie. "Once the time passed, I knew I should have called you to apologize, but I didn't want to admit my mistake, because I valued so much what you thought of me – oh, it's awful, I was so wrong all the way, tied up in knots . . . ."

Roy didn't interrupt Eddie's flood of genuine sorrow. He was pleased that Eddie now understood his error and was confident it wouldn't be repeated in the future. And, truth be told, Roy was a bit full of himself for how well he'd used the Madge Brody story to emphasize the value of truth-telling . . . .

"But Roy," said Eddie, who had now recovered from his admission of wrongdoing, "there is something I would like to know related to Madge."

Roy, a little surprised, said, "Sure, Eddie, what's that?"

"It's whether you have seen Madge since that day. Did you ever show her the resulting street pictures? Did you ask her if her nephew enjoyed the meal that evening? Have you let her tell you about the days when she was teaching school? Madge sounds like a wonderful woman – but other than her role in the story, does she mean anything to you?"

Eddie's words took Roy's breath away. He realized that he had done none of those things. He came away from the encounter with some good post-snowstorm photos and a story to tell – including its moral that he'd conveyed to

Eddie. But how about Madge Brody herself – where was his feeling for this remarkable woman? What happened to his own humanity?

He thought about Madge Brody's "photographic eye." What kind of "eye" did he have? A "literary" one, of course. A "moral" one, he hoped. But maybe not as much of a "compassionate" one as he would like to have.

I'm confident Eddie learned from the story, thought Roy – *but now, at long last, so have I.*

* * *

A woman named Clarissa was a regular in Roy's class from the first day. She was well-read, seemingly intelligent, and participated actively in the class. Roy appreciated students like Clarissa who raised pertinent questions about the assignments.

By way of example, at one early class on Emily Dickenson, Roy had said: "Dickenson excelled at explosive first lines that draw the reader in – for instance, 'My life had stood – a loaded gun' is one of her strongest openers."

Clarissa raised her hand and said, "But the poem is cryptic – maybe about the afterlife, maybe about an actual lover, maybe a meditation on anger, helplessness and power."

"You're so right, Clarissa," said Roy. "But Dickenson's answer came in another poem: 'Tell all the truth. – but tell it slant.' What does she mean? The last lines explain: 'The Truth must dazzle gradually or ever man be blind' – in other words, let the reader slowly grasp your meaning."

It should have been obvious to him, though, that Clarissa had more on her mind than fiction and poetry – in fact, she had Roy directly in her sights, and spoke about him to other residents in a manner that suggested the two of them were conducting an affair, even though nothing of the sort was taking place.

Roy was blissfully unaware of this, but one day he noticed that Brenda was acting coolly toward him. When it began to bother him, he raised the issue with her, trying to find out what, if anything, was wrong.

"What's wrong," she said quite bluntly, "is that you seem to be conducting an affair with a lady who isn't me."

Roy was instantly shocked by this false charge and demanded to know what she had heard. He rejected the charge in no uncertain terms. When Brenda seemed dubious about accepting his denial, he responded with immense heat: "Haven't I done enough to earn your trust?" At this point she threw her arms around him and whispered in his ear, "I'm so glad it isn't true."

When they finally disengaged after some loving moments, Brenda asked him, "But Roy, how do we get her to stop spreading that awful rumor?"

Roy replied instantly in an angry tone. "I'm just going to tell Clarissa to shut her goddamn mouth!"

"No," said Brenda. "Wait a minute – let's talk this over."

Roy sputtered briefly, but then cooled down. "Okay, we need to devise a strategy. First of all, how did that false report come to you? Was it directly from Clarissa?"

"No it didn't. I know who Clarissa is from seeing her in your class, but I've never even met the woman! The report came from a woman I do know, but don't like very much, named Ethel. She said – or at least certainly implied – that she had heard it directly from Clarissa."

Roy pondered the situation. "So we don't know exactly what Clarissa has been saying, or how specific she was. Maybe she just hinted at the relationship, and it was this Ethel who decided to blow it up into a full-scale affair."

"That's right," Brenda replied. "Sure, I want it cut it off completely, but since we don't know for sure what Clarissa said, there may be no reason to make an enemy of her." She paused for a few moments and then said, "I'm starting to get an idea of how we should handle it . . . ."

The next day, Roy arranged for the two of them to meet with Clarissa in Elmwood's spacious living room. Roy introduced the women: "Clarissa, this is Brenda, the woman I'm in love with and who has become a crucial part of my life. Brenda, this is Clarissa, who is a star student in my English class."

The two of them quietly acknowledged each other. Brenda then said, "Clarissa, I'm afraid that someone is taking your name in vain – making untrue allegations that you and Roy are engaged in a sexual affair. A rumor to that effect has come to my attention and, needless to say, has made me very unhappy."

Before Clarissa could reply, Roy said, "My guess, Clarissa, is that the person spreading that ugly rumor extrapolated our non-existent affair from the lively dialogue we frequently have in my class – a dialogue which, by the way, I really enjoy and hope to continue. But since my relationship with you doesn't in fact extend beyond the class, both Brenda and I would very much appreciate you issuing a clear denial if you become aware of any such rumor."

They didn't wait for a reply or question Clarissa but promptly excused themselves. Brenda said, 'Nice to meet you' on the way out and left Clarissa alone in the room. When Roy and Brenda arrived back in Brenda's apartment, they hugged and smiled, quite content that they would never be bothered by that rumor again.

* * *

The next day, they were seated at the dining table in Brenda's apartment, finishing off the remains of a light snack.

"Brenda," said Roy, "I hope you'll be able to come to my English class tomorrow – it should be fun. I'm going to talk about one of my favorite authors, Lewis Carroll."

She replied, "Oh, I wouldn't miss it – I grew up reading and re-reading *Alice in Wonderland* and *Through the Looking Glass*."

Roy, pleased by her response, felt himself so fortunate to have fallen in love with an ideal woman who shared his enthusiasm for good literature.

"I've had Eddie photocopy some of my favorite tidbits from those remarkable pages, which I'll be passing out to the attendees. For instance" – and here he handed Brenda a page containing one of the excerpts – "this is one of my favorite dialogues between Alice and the White Knight in *Looking Glass*. Please read the 'little box' bit out loud for me. If I can't memorize it, I may ask you in class to recite it aloud to the group.

Brenda scanned the page and then read it aloud:

"I see you're admiring my little box," the Knight said in a friendly tone. "It's my own invention – to keep clothes and sandwiches in. You see I carry it upside-down, so that the rain can't get in."

"But the things can get *out*," Alice gently remarked. "Do you know the lid's open?"

"I didn't know it," the Knight said, a shade of vexation passing over his face.

"Then all the things must have fallen out! And the box is no use without them."

Roy chuckled. "Don't you love it?! And the point it makes – well, it would serve as a wonderful epigraph for a book on the Japanese capture of Singapore in World War II, where all the British guns were trained on the sea – unable to be turned around – while the Japanese marched down the Malay Peninsula from the opposite direction without opposition."

Brenda nodded in agreement and said, "It reminds me of when the White Knight says to Alice "you've got to be prepared for everything" and he points to the anklets around the feet of his horse. She asks him what those are for, and he tells her, "To guard against the bite of sharks"."

"Oh that's a good one." said Roy "But listen to me recite my favorite, which I memorized a long time ago. It's the White Knight telling Alice the new way he had invented of getting over a gate.

"You see, I said to myself 'The only difficulty is with the feet; the head is high enough already.' Now, first I put my head on the top of the gate – then the head's high enough – then I stand on my head – then the feet are high enough, you see – then I'm over, you see."

Brenda laughed. "That's a real winner. And how about when Alice encounters the Unicorn. Each of them admits to having thought the other was a fabulous monster, and then the Unicorn says, "Well now that we have seen each other, if you'll believe in me, I'll believe in you'."

"Right on!" said Roy. "And here's just one more I've memorized – the advice to Alice spoken by the Duchess in *Alice in Wonderland.*

. . . "Be what you would seem to be – or, if you'd like it put more simply – never imagine yourself not to be otherwise than what it might appear to others that what you were or might have been was not otherwise than what you had been would have appeared to them to be otherwise."

Roy continued. "And then when Alice says she can't quite follow it, and the Duchess says, "that's nothing to what I could say if I chose,' I love Alice's reply: "Pray don't trouble yourself to say it any longer than that."

Brenda stood up, went over to Roy, kissed him on the cheek, and said, "I just can't wait for the class."

* * *

Later that day, inspired by their frolic with Lewis Carroll's prose, Brenda said to Roy, "Did I ever tell you about my friend John?"

"No, I don't recall that you did."

"Well," said Brenda," one day John decided that life would be much easier if he had a clone. He has one made and sends him to work while he stays home and relaxes. But this backfires one day when the clone comes home and tells John that he has been fired for making sexual advances to women in the office."

"Excuse me," said Roy, but where is this going?"

Brenda ignored his interruption. "So John decides he has to get rid of his clone. He takes it to the top of a tall building and pushes it off. Unfortunately, someone sees John do this, and he's arrested for the crime of *making an obscene clone fall.*"

There was silence for a moment, and then Roy let out a groan. "Oh my God, I had no idea where you were going with that one – arrested for making an *obscene clone fall* – now that's real wordplay."

Brenda smiled and said, "I thought you might like one of these – even though your English teacher background probably regards a punch line like that as repellent."

"Oh, does it?" asks Roy. "Well, I just happen to have one of these of my own."

"Come on," said Brenda, "I can't imagine such a distortion of the mother tongue coming from you."

"Well just listen," said Roy. "A group of chess enthusiasts are standing in a hotel lobby discussing tournament victories. After an hour, the manager comes by and asks them to go to their rooms.

"But why?" they ask, as they prepare to move off.

The manager replies. "Because I just I can't stand *chess nuts boasting in an open foyer."*

Now it was Brenda's turn to groan, which she followed up with, "Roy, I'm so glad I underestimated you here," punctuated by a kiss on his cheek.

It was clear that things were going well for them. The threats posed by Clarissa and Larry Owen had been disposed of. Roy would have proposed marriage already if he hadn't been concerned that Bob's relatives or some Elmwood residents might consider this to be too soon after Bob's passing. The road ahead looked broad and bright.

THE STRUGGLE

A week later, when Eddie arrived for their daily session, all traces of Roy's playfulness and joy had vanished, leaving him a man depressed almost to the point of despondency.

Eddie was startled by the transformation. "What's wrong, Roy? You were so upbeat the last time I saw you. Why the long face now? Are you and Brenda having a problem?"

"There's no problem between us – we're very much in love. But something new has come up and it may ruin everything."

"What happened? Tell me – maybe I can help."

Roy took a sip of water before addressing the new problem he found so painful. "I may not have mentioned it to you, but Brenda has a son, Peter, from a brief marriage in her early 20's. He lives with his wife and kids in northern Minnesota. Up to now he hasn't been playing a big role in her life – other than picking up part of the tab for her living expenses. He didn't even attend Bob's funeral. But now, it seems, Peter wants to make up for his past neglect."

"How so?"

"The son-of-a-gun has invited his mother to come out to northern Minnesota and live with him and his family! He says he wasn't able to do that while her husband was alive – Bob's dementia would have been too much for the family to handle – but now that Brenda is alone, Peter would like to have her join them. He wants his children to get to know their grandmother – you know, the whole nine yards."

"What's Brenda's reaction?" Eddie asked.

"She's torn. She professes to love me, but I'm a new factor in her life. Peter goes all the way back – and the idea of getting to know her grandchildren better holds some appeal."

"Do you think she might actually go?"

"Yes, I do. That's what has me so demoralized. Just when I found the love of my life, I may be about to lose her. We would already be married if we hadn't decided to wait out of respect for Bob."

Eddie's voice took on a positive tone. "Hey, don't give up the ship, Roy. This calls for a strategy to keep Brenda here. I'm already getting a few ideas...."

"I hope you can think of something – I've run out of ideas."

"I'm on it, Roy. But one thing I can tell you right now – the way to keep Brenda here is to make her realize how much her leaving Elmwood would hurt *you*."

Roy's mind flashed back to the vow he had made so many years ago after college – a pledge not to play on anyone else's pity to achieve ends of his own.

Roy's response was prompt and firm. "No, Eddie, I won't do that. I don't want to take advantage of whatever sympathy she has for me. We've got to devise some other tactics...."

* * *

"I have something here for you," said Roy the next day, when Brenda answered his knock on her door.

"What is it?" she asked, puzzled by the earmuffs he was wearing indoors.

"Here, look," he said, thrusting a piece of paper into her hand with a theatrical gesture. "It's today's daily weather report from northern Minnesota – a real blizzard, 15 inches of snow, temperature at 20 below zero, winds of 30 miles per hour."

Brenda replied wearily, "I know, I know."

"Not only that," Roy added. "Do you know that they have 14,000 lakes out there; and when it's not snowing, like mainly in the summer, they have about 14,000 mosquitos per lake. Plus which, they're not little guys – some are so big they carry away small children."

"Okay, okay," said Brenda in mock exasperation – "I get it"

Roy persevered. "And by the way, there's a large Scandinavian and German population out there. Very stoic people. I've heard that there was a Minnesotan father who loved his son so much that he almost told him."

Brenda smiled weakly, and Roy felt that his point – such as it was – had been made.

* * *

Later that afternoon, Eddie inquired about it. "How did Brenda react today when you reported on the Minnesota weather?"

Roy shrugged. "Well, she said something like, 'I know, I know, it's terrible' – an observation in which I heartily concurred. It was a good idea, Eddie, and I thank you for coming up with the concept; but frankly, I don't think the weather will be enough to keep her from heading west."

"Don't worry, Roy – it's all cumulative, and I've got another plan up my sleeve."

* * *

"Yes, they're good-looking kids," Roy said to Brenda the next day. They were sitting at her kitchen table, viewing photos of her grandchildren that she kept in an album. "And Peter may well be an admirable son, at least at a distance."

Roy paused a beat before firing his big gun, courtesy of Eddie's latest brainstorm. "But Brenda, here's what you have to consider – and that's Peter's wife, Donna. You almost never mention her, which leads me to believe she's not one of your favorite people. And you'd be moving into *Donna's* house. She's likely to resent your constant presence, afraid you'll be second-guessing the way she runs the household and brings up her kids. You're going to represent a real threat to her dominion . . . ."

* * *

"What's new on the Brenda front?" asked Eddie the next Monday upon his arrival in Roy's room.

"It's like a roller coaster," replied Roy. "I was making real progress with her. She recognized Peter's wife as a serious potential problem. For the first time, she did raise with Peter the notion of her staying here."

"That's great."

"But try to guess how he replied? He said it was out of the question – and not just because he and his family wanted Brenda to live with them. No, now he cited 'financial reasons' for his insistence on her making the move."

"Oh, I don't like the sound of that."

"Peter told her that paying for her room and board at Elmwood had become too much of a burden on his modest income, without the contribution he'd been receiving from Bob's pension, which expired on his death. In short, he insisted that he needs to save money by having her join them."

"Aha," said Eddie, "that may have been his motive all along. You can actually use that with Brenda against her precious son."

"Maybe so, but here's the rub – if he's cruel enough to cut her off financially, she won't be able to afford to stay here."

"Let's talk about that – I've already got a thought on the subject . . . ."

* * *

THE RESOLUTION

"Brenda, darling, I figured it out" Roy said to her over lunch the next day. "We can make it financially here without Peter's help. I can move in with you – the space is big enough for the two of us – and by saving the money I've been paying Elmwood for my room and scraping together a few other dollars, we should be able to make out okay. . . ."

"Oh, Roy, that sounds like it may be possible . . . ."

* * *

But when Eddie arrived for their session a few days later, Roy was once again downcast.

"I tried everything, Eddie – even the financial argument, although you know I have some doubts about my ability to swing that deal. But it looks like I've failed. She's getting ready to leave for Minnesota in less than a week."

"I thought she loved you."

"I think she still does. . . although in addition to saying he wouldn't support her, Peter has also been chipping away at that."

"How so?"

"When Brenda told him that I was the reason she wanted to stay at Elmwood, do you know what he said?"

"What?"

"Brenda didn't want to tell me, but I pressed her. She finally revealed that Peter said something along these lines: 'This guy Roy is too old for you; he's losing his sight, so you'll have to care for him like you did for Bob; he has no money – he's just a superannuated ex-high school English teacher' – as if that were something ignoble."

Eddie exploded. 'Why that son of a gun!" When he calmed down, he realized he wasn't ready to give up the fight. "You say you've tried everything, Roy, but have you told Brenda how much her leaving would hurt *you*?"

Roy's reply was calm but firm. "No, I haven't. But as I told you before, I refuse to play on her sympathies. . . ."

* * *

Late that evening after his classes, Eddie stopped for a beer at a neighborhood tavern. Sitting alone at the bar nursing a cold brew, he mused over Roy's problem.

Roy is making a big mistake, Eddie thought, in refusing to let Brenda know how much her departure would hurt him. *That's the one bit of leverage he has to use to keep her from leaving.*

Eddie didn't want to go directly against Roy's wishes, but he pondered whether there was some way to get the point across to Brenda without violating what Roy was determined to avoid. A little tactical push, he thought, to get true love all the way home. And as he took a sip of his beer, the germ of an idea came to him.

But, he pondered, *would it work? And is it all right for me to – well, not exactly lie, but let's say, tell a half-truth? And should I be doing any of this when I haven't been asked to. . . ?*

Eddie continued to down his beer and give the situation some more thought. . . .

* * *

Roy lay quietly in his bed. It was Tuesday night, and Brenda was scheduled to leave for Minnesota the next morning. The idea of being with her this last day was just too painful for him, so he stayed alone in his apartment.

But he couldn't stop thinking about her and dwelling on the irony of the situation. *I had to wait for Bob to die before I could declare my love for Brenda. But it was the very fact of his death that is now being used as the reason for her having to leave me . . . . Whoever's arranging things upstairs has a twisted sense of humor . . . .*

He was about to turn out the light when he heard a knock. He got out of bed, opened the door, and there stood Brenda, radiant in a nightgown and robe. She smiled coquettishly and said, "May I come in?"

Roy was wary as she entered the room and led him over to the bed. Beckoning to Roy to get in, she climbed in alongside him. "Are you sure this is the way you want to spend our last night together?" he asked.

Brenda beamed as she spoke. "No . . . . But this is the way I want to spend the first of thousands of nights together with you . . . . I've decided to stay at Elmwood!"

Roy erupted in joy, and for the next few minutes the two of them hugged and kissed, whispered and laughed, and then hugged some more.

Later, when things had quieted down a bit, Roy said, "If you don't mind telling me, Brenda, why did you change your mind?"

Brenda, who obviously had anticipated the question, answered readily. "I don't mind telling you. Deciding to leave or stay was always a hard decision for me. What convinced me was a visit I had earlier this evening from your reader, Eddie."

Roy turned on his side to face Brenda. "Eddie? My Eddie went to see you? Why?"

"He wanted to get some advice from me, as your closest friend here, on how to handle a problem he had regarding you."

Roy seemed puzzled. "What advice?"

Brenda now turned on her side to face Roy. "I guess it's all right for me to pass along what he said. Well, although Eddie hasn't told you yet, he has applied to the state university – a school he'd like to attend and should be able to get in. But that will mean he won't be in town any longer, and he doesn't know how to break the news to you. He's well aware of how dependent you've become on all the assistance he offers you. Anyway, he thought I might be able to suggest the best way for him to raise the subject with you."

"And what did you tell him?"

Brenda reached over and gently touched Roy's face. "I told him go off to the state college, and I would take care of you."

"Huh?"

Brenda moved closer to Roy, her words resonating in his ear. "I've been so stupid, Roy – just thinking about myself. I never stopped to realize what effect my leaving Elmwood would have on *you* – the person I cherish most in the world."

She paused to brush his cheek with her lips. "I guess I overlooked this because you were always too much of a gentleman to bring it up. But you don't need Eddie to read to you – I can do that. You don't need to open a can of sardines for dinner – I'll cook for you. I can take you to places that are difficult for you to navigate with your AMD – concerts and theatre. And I'll take on some part-time work in the town library to help pay our expenses." She moved her body into contact with his. "And I can snuggle up with you at night just like this. . . ."

Roy's mind was on overload. He hadn't sought her sympathy, and he had to admit that Eddie had steered clear of it also – *but his pretext did have that effect, and was that a sound basis on which to move forward?*

"But Brenda, I don't want you to stay out of sympathy for me – "

"Don't worry, Roy. Now that I've made the decision, I realize I'm not doing it just for you, or just for me, but for both of us – we need each other."

Her answer was just what Roy wanted to hear, eradicating all doubts, and he finally relaxed.

"And Roy, just hear me cry – like in that *Gatsby* epigraph you hold so dear – 'Lover, gold-hatted, high-bouncing lover, I must have you. . . .'" Then, throwing her arms around him, she purred, "And now it's time for us to *really* celebrate the occasion. . . ."

* * *

When Eddie walked in the door the next day, Roy gave him a stern look and said, "Young man, I've got a bone to pick with you."

"Hold that a minute, Roy. I heard the good news that Brenda is staying at Elmwood – and realizing how much it means to you, I just want you to know how happy that makes me."

Roy pressed on, scowling as he spoke. "And that's precisely the subject I want to discuss. I've now learned that you went to see Brenda yesterday without my permission."

"Did I need your permission?"

"And contrary to my express avowal, you played on her sympathies."

"No, I didn't – I just asked her for advice as to what I should do about my education. If she made the jump from that to what *she* should do, well, she did it all by herself."

"And tell me this, young man – how can you justify that lie you told her about applying to the state college?"

"It wasn't a lie – just a half-truth. As a matter of fact, I've been thinking for months about doing this, but I didn't want to leave you high and dry. Now I'm over that. As a matter of fact, I have the completed application with me today – I want to ask you for a reference letter."

At this point, Roy dropped his pose of mock outrage, embracing Eddie in a big bear hug. "You're my boy. In fact, when Brenda and I get married next month, you'll be my best man."

The two of them clung to each other, in what could have passed for a warm father-son embrace.

A few moments later, Roy asked Eddie, "Tell me, Eddie what inspired you to do what you did?"

Eddie's face broke out into a big smile as he spoke. "Well, it really bothered me that your campaign to win over Brenda – or shall I say *our* campaign – which had been so successful earlier, was now about to crumble. And I remembered that quote of Napoleon you used with me so often, when I failed to finish what I'd begun – '*If you start to take Vienna – take Vienna!*' Right?"

Ray beamed. "Right! And by the way, *now* I can tell you what that high-bouncing *Gatsby* epigraph is all about...."

Made in the USA
Middletown, DE
17 November 2024

64403280R00040